mike kleine is a writer.
third world magicks is
his fifth book.

also by mike kleine

mastodon farm

arafat mountain

kanley stubrick

*the mystery of the seventeen pilot fish
(a play)*

Lonely men club

karaoke night at daisuke's

with dan hoy

*where the sky meets the ocean and the
air tastes like metal and the birds
don't make a sound*

we r the world

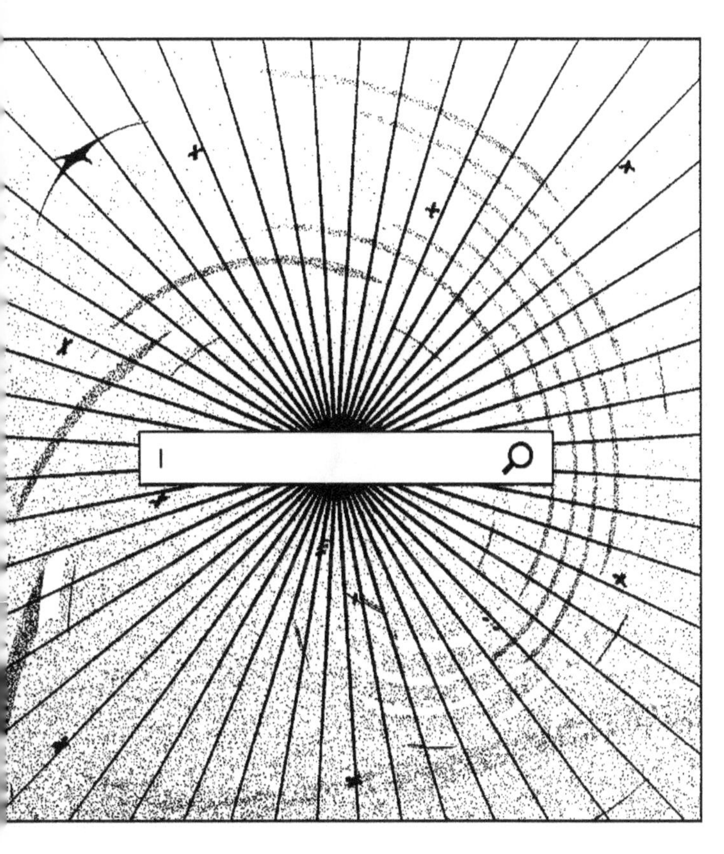

text is set in consolas, a
monospaced typeset designed (by
luc(as)de groot) as a replacement
for courier new. it is the only
standard windows os font with a
slash thru the zero character.

THIRD WORLD MAGICKS
written by MIKE KLEINE

INSIDE THE CASTLE
LAWRENCE, KS

second edition
copyright © 2022 mike kleine

this is a work of fiction. names, characters, places and incidents either are the product of the author's imagination or used fictitiously. any resemblance to actual persons, living or dead, events, or locales is entirely coincidental.

third world magicks is the 34th release from inside the castle.

thank you: john, john, jon, vi, ken, josiah, elle, amy and maman.

w w w . i n s i d e t h e c a s t l e . o r g
behind the façade, more of the same.

*for katherine &
lindsay & shawn*

*thank you for
everything*

"*[instrumental]*"

> —dean blunt and inga copeland,
> *1 (venice dreamway)*

"*flaws are discontinuities that act as tiny fissures, allowing the dim and distant, diffused gem light of pre-creation to slip thru — it is this that music existed for — a signpost, a reminder, a note.*"

> —rudy tambala / a.r. kane

"*L'enfer, ces les autres.*"

> —jean-paul sartre, *huis clos*

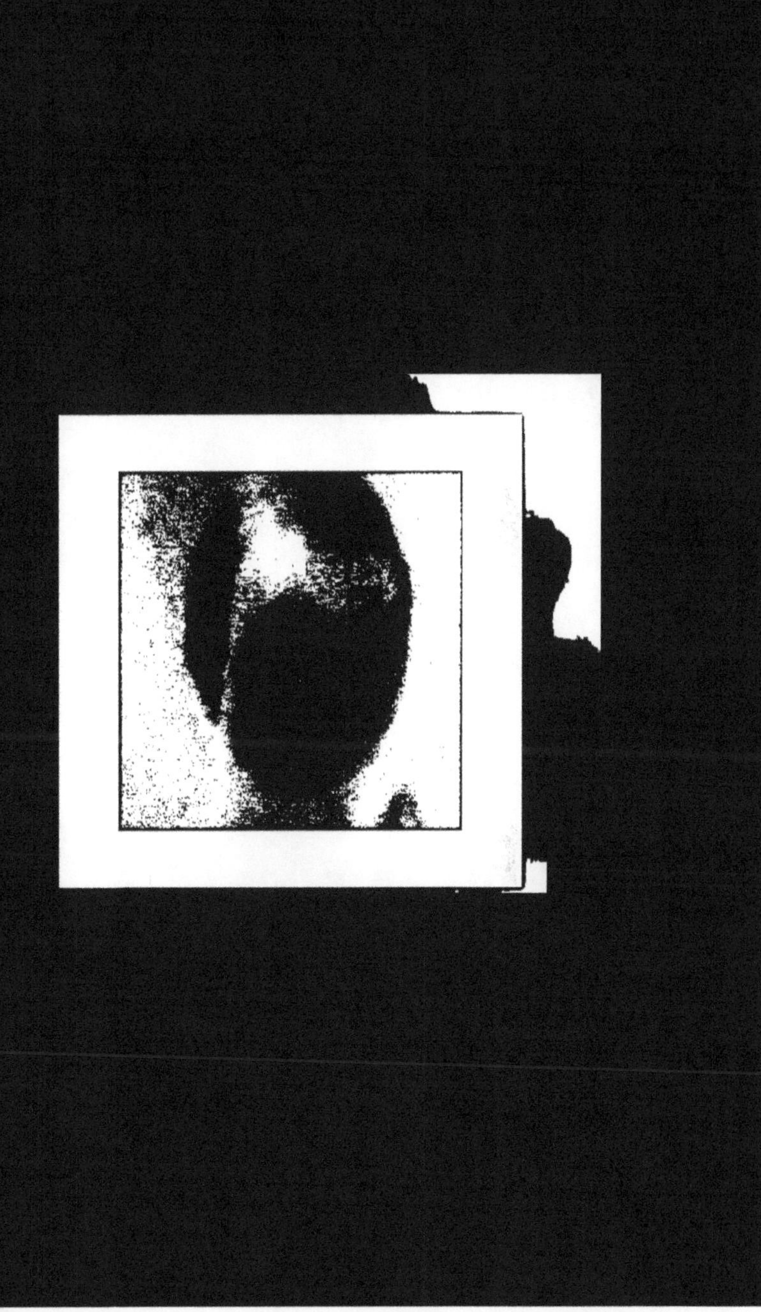

Find out what happens
when people stop being
polite, and start gettin real.

blank zizou is writing a long-form essay on klangfarbenmelodie.

she feels the article is either going to make or break her career.[*]

zizou submits the story to her editor, beach babi, and in the third paragraph of the body of the email, writes, *i really don't have much else to say. it's something i've been working on*

---

[*] professional music critic

for a very long time and feel like it's finally ready.

a few weeks go by.

eventually, the article is accepted, further edited, and published... but no one in the office really says anything about it.

(not even on the internet.)

zizou brings up, at a staff meeting the following week, that the article is something she worked on for a very long time.

beach babi addresses zizou and says, "it was good. seriously. well-written. nice job."

beach babi also says, pretty quickly, and to no one in particular, more, to the room, as if to totally avoid the subject or confrontation, "there's some obscure musician from serbia coming in this week — someone needs to write about him."

zizou, in that particular moment, feeling cheated and unwanted, becomes even more dissatisfied with herself and her job, because she believes the article should have been praised — or, at the very least, given more attention... maybe even featured on the front page of the magazine's website.

an hour passes.

after all the stories are taken, nobody, it turns out, is interested in writing about the obscure musician from serbia so, naturally, to look good in front of her boss (beach babi) and also, all of her co-workers, and to show that she is ready to do almost anything to succeed, zizou raises her hand and volunteers herself (even though she is already assigned two other articles:

1) a featurette on japanese noise artist, merzbow; and 2) an exhaustive 100 songs of the decade list (complete w/ personal commentary)).

beach babi looks at zizou and says, "zizou, thank you," and, "that's great" and, "you'll be writing with bloodrip.exe."

beach babi points to an entity sitting nearest to a window toward the back of the room.

at home, zizou discovers the music of the obscure musician from serbia on apple music and finds it to be terribly uninteresting, but at the same time, realises this is something she must do (in order to succeed).

zizou scours the net for articles (anything, really) but can't seem to find much information on the musician.

one person says, "this music will take you to another place," and another writes, "truly something to experience before you die."

zizou freaks out a little and has this mild panick attack — but that's normal and totally par for the course, because: that's what zizou does.

zizou stresses out some more and thinks about the rest of the week (even though it has not happened yet) and decides that not everything in life is always glamour and all glitz — much like the doctor at the doctor's office who is forced to answer mundane questions from ridiculous patients, day in and day out, or the cashier at the department store who is expected to smile for every single customer.

zizou decides that if she can tough it out for a few more years, make a few necessary sacrifices, and show that she is dedicated to what she is truly passionate about,[†] she will make a name for herself in the business, eventually, and maybe even fulfill her dream of meeting another truly great music writer.

someone to be with.

she is lucky, after all, (and zizou knows this all too well) to be writing for one of the top music magazines in the country, and besides, (after searching for and finding them on facebook) realises: bloodrip.exe is kind of cute.

[†] becoming a world-renowned music critic

it's a few days later.

they're riding a taxi, on their way to the show.

bloodrip.exe turns to zizou and says, "we'll need at least two quotes about the instruments. apparently, a bunch of them, abul mogard built himself. and then the rest is all just farfisa organ. i did some research on the internet. people really think that's neat. we need to talk about that."

zizou turns to bloodrip.exe and says,
"that is kind of neat, about the
farfisa organ," and thinks to herself,
*i really need to play it cool in
front of bloodrip.exe.*

they arrive to the place with the obscure musician from serbia.

the manager of the obscure musician from serbia greets bloodrip.exe and says to zizou, "abul mogard is in the upstairs dining room by himself so now, maybe, might be the best time to interview."

they head upstairs.

zizou shakes the hand of abul mogard
and asks if it's okay to take pictures.

the interpreter explains something to
abul mogard and abul mogard scratches
the top of his head and nods.

zizou takes a couple portrait shots
and then a handful of abul mogard
standing next to his instruments.

half an hour passes.

bloodrip.exe   asks   abul   mogard

questions about his upbringing, musical education, favourite time of year, upcoming projects, potential collaborations, sources of inspiration, favourite films, and of course, the instruments.

abul mogard doesn't say too much about himself or anything else really.

as a matter of fact, zizou finds most (if not all) of abul mogard's answers to be supremely dull & generic.

bloodrip.exe, at the end, says, "thank you," and excuses themself from the room.

zizou follows.

bloodrip.exe says, "i hope i asked enough relevant questions."

zizou says, "yeah, it's fine. i think you did. if you didn't, we'll figure something out, i'm sure."

zizou thinks, *still gotta play it cool in front of bloodrip.exe.*

it's a couple hours later and it's right before the show.

zizou heads downstairs to the bar and finds a woman with a face like fire and introduces herself and says, "i am writing an article on abul mogard for a music magazine."

the woman with the face like fire nods and explains to zizou that though it is certainly fascinating and interesting to have someone like an obscure musician from serbia come to perform at their concert venue, it is also not very lucrative for them and, "certainly bad for business. it's things like that that cause us to go out of business."

zizou says, "so, this is your place?"

the woman with the face like fire says, "me and the husband both," and tilts her head up, toward a man with eyes like the sky.

at the same place, directly below — downstairs, bloodrip.exe is interviewing a few of the attendees.

first, a man with ears like the galaxy, who says, "these sorts of things happen all the time — the obscure musician from some obscure place. and then all the local music magazines come to write up about him," and he points to bloodrip.exe's face, "because he's obscure. it does nothing for the community."

another man (this one, with a face like the moon,) says, "...the young people who pay to come and see these shows. watch, no one'll come to a show, but after your article publishes, we won't even be able to get mr. abul mogard to come back and perform in this town, ever again!"

in looking for bloodrip.exe, zizou goes back upstairs.

she finds abul mogard, his back to her, just standing there, all by himself.

his instruments are all gone and there's nothing left in the room.

abul mogard does not realise zizou is watching him.

he is positioned by one of the windows, caressing the nape of his neck, looking out into space.

zizou doesn't say anything and watches for a bit.

eventually, growing bored of this man (again), zizou quietly exits, and walks back downstairs.

zizou finds bloodrip.exe back at the bar, drinking, and talking to the woman with the face like fire.

they finish their conversation and the woman with the face like fire gets up to leave.

bloodrip.exe says, "how are things?"

zizou says, "do you mean with like, life or me or *just*," and points at her legs, "right now?"

bloodrip.exe laughs and says, "whatever you want."

zizou sits and orders drinks for the two of them and talks about grad school and the musicks of: tim hecker, m.c. mack, oneohtrix point never, ben frost, microstoria, JD TWITCH, the phantasy, kali malone, shinichi atobe, serpentwithfeet, holly herndon, danny brown, cube, dj punisher, aja, somi, rage against the machine, snail mail, jenny hval, dip in the pool, subjoi, trudge, actress, gene hunt, wu-tang clan, sunn o))), suzanne ciani, sd laika, harry forbes, philip glass, the national, slacker, aya, kuedo, lutto lento, turinn, sufjan stevens, the virgins, kelman duran, noriko miyamoto, beatrice dillon, konx-om-pax, mark guiliana, spirit of the beehive, PLANNINGTOROCK, terminal 11, don cherry, minimal violence, lightning bolt, tangerine dream, tim reaper, perfect mother, ill ease, XXXTentacion, cabaret voltaire, fuji|||||||||ta, phoebe bridgers, tems, mary lattimore, chavinski, teste, roly porter, ghostpoet, these new puritans, jamie xx, dj stingray, rxm reality, fjaak, mourning [a] BLKstar, fire-toolz, takami hasegawa, dawit eklund, cevdet erek, dehd, japandroids, lueke, jai paul, laurel halo, zomby, indigo de souza, mort garson, jlin, skander, robert cox, moist 96, intronaut, lcd soundsystem, boris, lomelda, mitski, i.b.m., björk, caroline polacheck, tom jarmey, lil baby, beat detectives, evan parker, grouper, wendy carlos, yaeji, the slits, j dilla, ethel cain, mf doom, william fields, aphex twin, duval timothy, amy dabbs, terrence dixon, dedekind cut, kaitlyn aurelia smith, john glacier, arpanet, gang gang dance, rina sawayama, rude ass tinker, gage, muqata'a, the zenmenn, have lyfe, wha ha ha, julian casablancas, joe hisaishi, la fraicheur, adrianne lenker, hara alonso, volodymyr bystriakov, zach hill, trent reznor & atticus ross, suicide, elsa hewitt, angelo badalamenti, moin, sonoko, kate nv, dj harlow, shygirl, bad bunny, francis bebeye, wanda group, senyawa, food pyramid, drakeo the ruler, sun kil moon, bd1982, angel bat dawid, dwight sykes, naoki asai, mats erlandsson, amnesia scanner, zipcode, toshifumi hinata, prince, burial, king crimson, yellow swans, lil' heavy, megan thee stallion, black midi, dogleg, lasse marhaug, bbc radiophonic workshop, greg fox, cevdet erek, tomaga, samsuo, hrdvsion, freddie gibbs & madlib, deerhunter, lyra pramuk, manisdron, remko scha, angel olsen, tony lugo, galaxy express 555, patrick belaga, lee gamble, rabit, ka, rogue state, ema, giant claw, glo phase, the soft pink truth, autechre, bill stone, soshi takeda, ye gods, grimes, koreless, jeff parker, sexores, moses sumney, playboi carti, aaron dilloway, east of eden, minor threat, kiwanoid, soccer mommy, fennesz, tom mudd, blood incantation, matana roberts, bbsitters club, u.s. girls, oceansize, lotic, fka twigs, fiona apple, panaché, the field, godspeed you! black emperor, mica levi, john maus, lucy gooch, d/p/i, gant-man, jessy lanza, fugazi, katya yonder, kenny larkin, ellll, visionist, joanna newsom, jun fukamachi, café alé, rbchmbrs, weniwasu, vangelis, shabazz places, huerco s., farrah abraham, merzbow, nonlocal forecast, the armed, kendrick lamar, chants, burna boy, yuri suzuki, oxbow, stars of the lid, haco, nr/ma, dj overdose, the raincoats, florian t m zeisig, kasbo, ross from friends, haruomi hosono, cd slopper, wobbly, special interest, king krule, jam city, glue boy, xen chron, the knife, klein, vegyn, jung frye, route 8, drexciya, SOPHIE, tirzah, dj rashad, tibslc, lorenzo senni, bogdan raczynski, quicksails, james blake, loveshadow, skullflower, pulse emitter, pantea, softcoresoft, pusha t, fax, dntel, mukqs, the gerogerigegege, kaleida, ariel pink, saloli, charli xcx, bartees strange, †, liquid son, rich gang, pink flag, bisk, lil uzi vert, yu su, prequel, roland ray, xenia rubinos, legowelt, andrew hung, the microphones, black bones, leonce, steve hauschildt, keiyaA, d'angelo, mdou moctar, navy blue, metal fingers, taped over memory, tommy wright iii, panda bear, kelly ruth, amen dunes, vatican shadow, frank ocean, indopan, half mortal, peder mannerfelt, l'rain, zane trow, mike shannon, bill callahan, jane inc, m. geddes gengras, saloli, the caretaker, supreems, cyborg 95, hailu mergia & the walias, dark0, lil noid, hidden spheres, infinite body, luc ferrari, titus andronicus, proswell, 18+, weyes blood, haim, senyawa, kara-lis coverdale, old tower, rainforest spiritual enslavement, wolves in the throne room, delroy edwards, john frusciante, skee mask, daft punk, kelly lee owens, emil beaulieau, roza roza, jim o'rourke, beau wanzer, rené najera, cherry stones, mint julep, hannah diamond, 100 gecs, andy stott, dj panthr, lawrence english, james ferraro, beach house, holy fuck, destroyer, eli keszler, recsund, elysia crampton, iokoi, steve reich, kero kero bonito, moor mother, ema, jakob ogawa, hexa, a.g. cook, princess nokia, clairo, sigillum s, THE HUMBLE BEE, loraine james, yan jun, young thug, fatima al qadiri, julia holter, death grips, zs, rafael anton irisarri, mj guider, pc music, innsyter, waxahatchee, john adams, liturgy, blair sound design, arca, jessie ware, amaarae, MIKE, big thief, porridge radio, inga copeland, aaron cupples, viagra boys, head kandi, salamanda, knocked loose, graham lambkin/jason lescalleet, autoerotichrist, equiknoxx, nubya garcia, bartees strange, king woman, omar suleyman, triad god, salem, macintosh plus, mount eerie, atom tm, bill orcutt, jon fay, nina kraviz, IDLES, louis cole, lil b, alan vega, fly pan am, clipping., yung lean, scott walker, sebastiAn, anz, yellow gas flames, yves tumor, june, nicolas jaar, laila sakini, star searchers, william basinski, chino amobi, lucy dacus, lorn, helen, thundercat and dean blunt, and how all of them are changing the world... how right now, she's also in the midst of researching minimal ambient music from the 20th century for a special feature she plans to write, later in the year.

bloodrip.exe says, "have you pitched it to beach babi yet?"

zizou says, "no. i think, maybe i might submit to another magazine."

bloodrip.exe says, "oh my."

zizou says, "i feel like it's maybe time to branch out."

bloodrip.exe says, "brave."

music starts.

the opener is some kid from japan. it's just him onstage, with an upright piano, effects pedals and seven microphones.

they watch from the bar.

zizou looks up the kid on her phone.

bloodrip.exe says they find the music to be kind of soothing.

zizou waits for the first song to finish and as people are clapping, continues with her story and delves into the specifics of how she spends most of her evenings watching youtube videos of mountains and saves dozens of pictures of mountains onto her laptop.

bloodrip.exe says, "what's the deal with the mountains?"

zizou says she believes mountains are linked to the energy and secrets of the cosmos.

she tells bloodrip.exe that her favourite mountain is mt. kilimanjaro and that she's been reading a lot of books and articles on quantum chromodynamics.

bloodrip.exe thinks about this for a bit and says, "i dunno what that is."

they[‡] change topics and talk, instead, about their pinterest boards, the seven instagram accounts they manage (for fun,) how life will always be a mystery to everyone and how they still do not know what they want to do for a career and how the whole music-writing thing, for them, is just an easy and quick thing (maybe).

zizou says, "what do you mean *quick*?"

bloodrip.exe says, "i mean, like, i like music and all that, just as much as the next person, but i could never see anyone writing about it for more than like, a couple years. seriously."

zizou makes a face and says, "i don't understand."

bloodrip.exe says, "everyone at the

[‡] bloodrip.exe

office, they're all like in their twenties or something. some are in their thirties, but like, mostly early thirties. y'know? i dunno. i mean. writing about music feels super transient to me. like, it's a stepping stone to something much greater. or, something, at least, that's much better. something else that you might really want to do."

zizou looks at bloodrip.exe and doesn't say anything.

as a matter of fact, looking at bloodrip.exe right now, zizou doesn't see anything (in them).

she thinks about the words and what they mean to her.

zizou thinks, *if i could no longer write about or talk about music — i think i might die.*

and it's at this specific moment, zizou realises, how she was wrong about bloodrip.exe.

she decides bloodrip.exe is no longer worth it.

bloodrip.exe says something about ear plugs and points to the stage (the opener — the kid from japan — is now done with his set).

people begin to gather in front of the stage.

abul mogard is about to play.

zizou stands and walks directly into the crowd.

bloodrip.exe calls for her and says something, like, *wait* or *where are you going.*

zizou doesn't pay attention.

she just keeps walking.

abul mogard appears around 11:16pm.

there's smoke and fog and haze and purple lights.

he begins his set with what zizou would later describe to beach babi as, "soft and simple music."

just floating farfisa organ sounds and scattered swatches of heavily reverbed pads. almost like a sound check. a lot of it, unassuming.

(let it be said,) zizou is not impressed.

and then it picks up... zizou realises that in a live setting, abul mogard's music is nothing like the apple music tracks she previewed.

the music becomes much more powerful. and immediate. visceral, even. almost palpable.

the music is loud and enormous.

onstage, abul mogard's setup is minimal.

you might never think a table with just a handful of custom synths, a farfisa organ, some cassette decks and a few effects pedals could produce such great sounds.

zizou stares hard at abul mogard.

compared to a more dynamic performance, from like, say, a rock & roll band or even a full orchestra, watching one man on stage for something like ninety minutes, just pushing buttons and turning knobs might seem like an uninteresting activity to the layperson... but to zizou(?), this was heaven:

the cold

, , ,   electro
         -nic blips   , , ,

         the distant
             ambient washes

         the high definition   ,
                 surround-sound   .
                     atmospherics   ,
                     ...
the languid   ...

                    synth   .   swells
        ,   ,
              the deep-bass rumblings
of   ,   the farfisa organ   .

                            the over-saturated
    .tape   .   .   hiss
    .   .
        the drippy   .
              cavernous   ,
                                  echoes
    .   .
              .
    ,
              .   the other-worldly
                    wind chime
                            sounds

        the hazy   ,   ,   ,   ,
        buzz-z-zzz-z-z-ing . . . effects
        .   .   .   .

          the hushed murmur and din
      .   .   of unintelligible
      .   .   human voices and
      .   . side-conversations
      .   . (happening, at all-
      .   .   .   .   times)
  ,
   `   ,   ,
  ,

      the waves
  of   static

           .

      .   . .

                             ,

           .   .   .

.   .

            ,

                              .

    ,   .

                    .

            .   . .

                              ,

        ,

                        .

                    ,

                        .   .

.   .

        .

it doesn't matter to zizou anymore
what anyone has to say about music.

abul mogard is a prophet!

she closes her eyes and succumbs to
the ambiance of it all.

it's at this point, zizou begins
to experience a moment of higher
consciousness.

albumin particulates drip down to
the floor... into the pores of high-
strength fortress concrete.

zizou heavy-glides over atomic
elements of bilirubin, guanidine and
mucoproteins.

she wobbles toward a spire structure,
all crystal shards tumbling from out
of an imagined sky.

a[n] sharp ambient haze manifests,
erasing and eviscerating *everything*,

all in real-time.

ambient occlusions, distant sculptures. reality unglued.

the bright-muted clank of heavenly gems.

the shatter dome, reduced to nothing.

shadow people.

a proto-terror blimp. throw-away components and techno-computer parts, from a bygone era.

the *worst* type of acid rain.

zizou's calico shirt dissolves and ruptures from within (on a yocto-level), melting and intertwining with the mocado and twill weave (of her coat jacket), as ruby-tinged and translucent body fluids jettison out and pierce the night-blue sky.

zizou phazes for a moment, and thinks about the universe, her essay, about her interminable desire for recognition, about her unrequited love for all things music, her passion for deep research, about all her failings and abandoned projects, her broken dreams, her student loans, her noticeable lisp, her receding hairline and about everything bloodrip.exe said.

a space beyond the black void of time, devoid of mosquito noises and smoke air, collapses to another corner of even more black void.

the clinking of silver objects in an abject hole. drifting thru the surface of a(n) crushed earth.

disrupting flows of stagnation that increase with audible intervals from an irregular sort of blood chant (w/ periodic glints of bright flash from reflective lunar metals).

rusted steel objects propped against an age-d building, peaking with prisms and tesseracts, the heavens overcast with a(n) washed-out orange-red ambient glow.

the stench of ambient decay.

stairs that lead to a place overflowing with blood bricks and chemical soot.

meat hooks refracting the syrup'd blue-grey light of a(n) dust'd-out moon.

in the stillness of absolute dimness, cavern'd rocks shifting invisibly, as if the absence of any sort of discernable light might allow for the nigh-impossible to occur.

soul-windows peer into the empire of zizou. her spine is ripped forward, as her nothing body follows.

the long shadow of a structure containing wood pulps and broken-down vr synthetics, infused with gelling-like skin cultures and *found*earth pittings from an obscure'd origin.

high-pitched squeals, a pink ray to the brain. the homicide-blue tinge of the way the leaves of the forest look at night, in some parts of the world.

the constant asphyxias, of clothes sewn from an irregular cut, meant to assuage the forever anxieties and horrors of modern *life*.

languishing behind person-sized mirrors, placed in the centre of an unexpected clearing, within the dense foliage of a[n] place no one should ever have to visit. a matte-black canvas.

the trouble with all of this, appears once the sun departs and all that remains, are the visible anti-aliased edges of a(n) traumatized irreality.

violent and horrifying end-results, forever entombed within the must'd-out recesses of a weak mind.

perfect diagrams producing angular shapes jutting out at strange angles, emblematically slashing the night sky, with slants and doses of oozing liquids.

the dropped sphere-box — the one from

out of the sky.

a lazy helicopter reveals itself, moments before the climax, the chop-chop sound, disturbing that which lies dormant, at the bottom of a cave.

zizou sees planets, a parallel universe with colours extending far beyond the human visual spectrum, a place that should not exist (where zizou and everyone else is made of shiny metals and archaic circuitry). images upon images of broken statuettes and floor plans of destroyed museums.

fragmented peninsulas and disrupted kettle lakes. an agonising crawl toward a(n) toxic muck. mystic lava lakes. cherubic fountains of youth.

zizou floats thru invisible molecules and sub-atomic virtual particles, creating waves of bladed erasure, slicing quazomes of potential'd air, reducing quarks into even more miniscule'd shreds of deep-fat-rendered and benign dark edge-materials.

zizou sees the beginning of *time*, hears planets explode, witnesses black holes disappearing (and then reappearing), more planets exploding, moons and atmospheres and stratus clouds forming, cyclonopedic dust storms and undiscovered pressure systems and earthquakes, tsunamis and interminable warp barriers.

zizou tries to open her eyes, in an attempt (albeit futile) to escape these (to her) terrible *visions*, (as she now feels as if she is about to have another panick attack) but all zizou can see when she opens her eyes, is fire and smoke and clouds and dust and bright lights.

oceans are burning.

she closes her eyes again, and is transported to (even) more distant places.

zizou finds herself on a purple-grey planet, plinking dulcet tones on a version of a version of a version of a nonlinear labs c15.

the sound is muffled and not overly bright. it is stiff, at first, but then travels more smoothly, gliding over (and thru) an ancient [ruin] kopje, gently agitating and roiling the fluids from a(n) nearby nameless lake.

faded arpeggio sounds reverberate

against the muted-orange chalk face of three centuries-old buttes.

in the distance, there exists a singular bronze-age gargantua monolith.

zizou records a few new-age sounds directly in front of the rockface.

she inserts a contact mic near a lava neck and captures the sounds of suffused magma, deep within the planet's crust.

next, on what feels (to zizou) to be a more gaseous planet, she loops dozens of soft water sounds she's programmed onto a deckard's dream mk2, using 4/5 time.

the amalgam is truly entrancing.

some of the natural reverb, from the

landscape, transforms a sense of great overflow into a(n) more palatable, self-modulating and closer-to-real-life sort of replication of semi-geyser-like sounds.

zizou sees herself floating over a mysterious giant *void*hole version of a[n] primordial grotto.

a rudimentary choir chant patch is launched into the cave's abyss, almost immediately returning with great and violent force; acting as piercing-like dagger-stabs of dissonant ambiance, mutated by the slick architectures of a(n) (already) (un)natural habitat.

the sun appears zonked, in a crude and metameric sky.

no sound of birds or any other brand of natural din/ambiance.

it's sepulchral silence.

not too far away, a burn pit with moon-markings left in the dirt.

the matte-black canvas of a[n] earthen sea, serving as transmogrified backdrop to a[n] psychic'd midi composition.

the lurch of a roland jv-1010 dark bass tone, enveloping several mood-pieces into a[n] sort of abstract digital atrifact'd abject (un)safe-space-made horror.

a new expansion card loaded, promising pan pipe sounds and medieval flute samples.

this particular sequence, for zizou, brings forth images and sequences of birds materialising from out of trees and azure blue waterfalls, all of

this, adding to a[n] already turgid
artificiality of x'd out bliss.

zizou feels intense spaghettification.

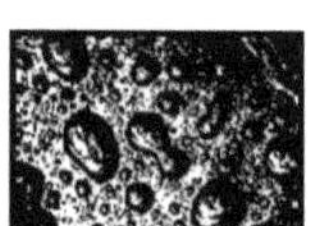

zizou is insta-warped back to supra-
reality.

human self-consciousness.

exiting sub-bass and the end-sounds
of concert music.

pure static energy, empty low fidelity
distorted cassette tape modulations
and the intermittent sound of a
crackling fog horn... warbled and
masked and obfuscated, by sheets
and sheets of dense soft-pink and

suffocating white noise.

zizou feels like she can't breathe.

she grabs at her face because it hurts so much.

abul mogard bows to the crowd.

zizou looks up. she feels abject terror.

abul mogard says something (but she can't hear it).

zizou is a neutron star.

zizou cries.[1]

on monday, beach babi reads the article and scans the quotes and says, "these are really good. i am very pleased." she asks bloodrip.exe, "how was the show?"

bloodrip.exe says that most of the people at the concert were either writers or photographers — "there weren't many *real* people at the show."

zizou says, "the show was incredible. he played a lot of his earlier pieces.

i liked the song 'the room' best."

beach babi says to bloodrip.exe, "that's normal, these sorts of things; that's what we do! we dictate what's *cool*," and then, to zizou, "great!"

beach babi puts a checkmark by the story 'obscure musician from serbia', on the whiteboard.

bloodrip.exe turns to zizou and says, "i liked the song he did after 'the room' the most i think, 'the sky had vanished' it was called."

zizou thinks about this and feels, for whatever reason, the need to be confrontational, and says, "actually, he played 'the other room' after 'the room', not 'the sky had vanished'."

"oh, i thought 'android manouvres'

came after 'the room'?"

"no, that was 'drooping off' and then 'staring at the sweeps of the desert', after 'the room'."

zizou thinks the following:

i do not care about bloodrip.exe.

i do not respect bloodrip.exe or their opinion about anything.

bloodrip.exe is dead and useless to me.

nothing they say matters or is important because they are not a true artist.

bloodrip.exe is here only because they know how to take advantage of other people.

bloodrip.exe has no vision because

they are a terrible person and the universe will never care about them or anything they have to say.

bloodrip.exe is a waste of anybody's time.

nobody should ever care about bloodrip.exe.

bloodrip.exe equals less than zero.

as bloodrip.exe is walking back to their desk, zizou alt-tabs back to whatever she was doing before the meeting, closes it and opens the link to her published article on klangfarbenmelodie and, using a completely made-up disqus account name, writes:

I find out what happens
when people stop being
polite, and start gettin real.

*please
wait 2 weeks
b4 reading
further*

thanks
4
waiting

as long as ropes unravel
fake rolex will travel.

black magician[2] appeared in late july,
when the sky was still a cornflower
blue & the earth rumblings stopped.

he ate half-steamed escargots & spoke
of published books & of academic lyfe
& provided instruction on how to
become a better person.

black magician also did this thing
with his h&s.

he drank whiskeys & smoked djarum
blacks & said things like, "white

cube is something new & wondrous that will never happen again."

black magician would usually pause & then continue, "because we are in an important moment in time right now, where limitations & regulations cannot affect the kind of world-changing work we are doing, literally, the sky is the limit."

after that, the earth rumblings would come back for a little bit, but with less frequency.

at night, black magician would recite poetry & sleep by the pond & play guitar & spend the better part of his days photographing plant lyfe & investigating rock formations near & around the white cube construxion site.

but not once did black magician take a picture of white cube or anything around white cube.

"it's because i cannot look directly at it," black magician explained. "the thing is, anything made of white magicks & the like —" & he pointed to white cube, "is much too wondrous & magnificent for me to even know what to do with."

black magician asked marfa preitzborne-huffer what she thought of white cube.

"i don't know," she said. "my mind does not think of things like that."

marfa preitzborne-huffer, see, her purpose was to identify light leaks & fume compounds, & then nothing else.

black magician respected that & knew
he had already said too much so he
stayed for another three (maybe four)
hours & then took off on a specially
designed yacht, made of (some of)
earth's rarest materials: holmium,
samarium & a bit of ytterbium.

but before he left, black magician
looked back & said, to a few of us,
"don't mind the light, it really is
just false promises & a whole lot of
kumbaya after that."

simonette de gaulle wrote down what
black magician had said & by the time
she finished & looked up, just like
that, he was gone.

constantinople de renobles eventually contracted pulmonary embolism & santiago jules shook his head & said, "that's because he works in the quartz mines."

it was during one of the lunch hours that constantinople de renobles coughed up syrupy blood & freaked everyone out. sallie umberto got some blood on her top & screamed, "surely, it's the end for me!"

the following evening, a doctor appeared on a slightly antiquated moped.

he wore light grey hartford slim-fit cotton trousers & a mauve marc jacobs bamboo-print crepe shirt.

his hair was neatly combed & loosely crimped & even in the august heat, not a drop of sweat could be seen on any part of his face.

susanna reauchambaud remarked,

"remarkable."

the doctor introduced himself as achilles yorembein & gave a speech on the dangers of working in the mines & scuba diving at night.

he told sallie umberto she would be safe. constantinople de renobles however, "that's a different story..." he said.

constantinople de renobles died that same evening.

we stopped work 4 the rest of the week & took time to celebrate his lyfe, "because that's what he would have wanted," san marita de renobles (constantinople de renobles' third wyfe) said.

the moment it happened, when constantinople de renobles finally reached the end of his lyfe, it is said the ghost of his soul could be seen leaving the body. as a result, alexia martène did a sign of the cross & jossua primm cried.

patrique barnaby, our spectroscopist, said, "if black magician had been here, he would have been able to save him."

eventually, the death of constantiople de renobles became but a distant memory. matthieu van der strijt planted a few palm trees in remembrance, but that was pretty much it.

marques framberk, overcome by a sudden depression & acute anxiety, threatened to quit because he felt he could find a better salary elsewhere.

giancarlo daviici, the workplace efficiency consultant, appeared from behind a sphere & said, "marques framberk, you are the total gas containment expert. you are the only total gas containment expert we have on this isl&. without you, who will educate us about total gas containment?"

marques franmberk remained silent.

giancarlo daviici then pointed to charlie francis. "charlie francis is our broken glass housewares specialist. we need him just as much as we need you. if you leave, you will be ab&oning us all."

marques framberk grumbled something & then returned to work.

that evening, at the campfire, after a dinner of roasted peppers, curried shrimp & garlic purée, someone told the story of constantiople de renobles & the rubber tree.

meanwhile, the foreman called marques
franmberk into his office to let him
know he had earned himself a 0.03€
raise.

the thing is, everyone here was just
as important as everyone else. without
one person, we were no person.

we completed white cube on a tuesday afternoon sometime in october.

white cube's colourway was a simple mix of two parts cosmic latte & one part anti-flash white.

but in this light, it looked almost pure white.

it wasn't long before men in suits began to appear, followed by women in expensive dresses — of all colours, shapes & sizes.

it was something of a spectacle.

there was a lot of commotion too, but also, to go with that, a lot of laughter.

the foreman told us, "go wear your best clothes. there's going to be pictures & after this, you'll be famous everywhere. every single one of you."

tareeq gamm measured all of the women & bertrand yamasaki, the men.

by evening, everyone had a custom outfit.

news crews arrived from around everywhere.

one reporter said he had flown all the way from canada & another lady said she'd missed her flight but made a deal with a[n] afrofuturist from kentucky & was lucky to have gotten here as quickly as she had.

a man named pippin quell coached us on what we were allowed to say & what we were not allowed to say.

we were h&ed documents we had to sign.

pippin quell said, "memorise these questions & then memorise the answers, too. do not memorise both at the same time; you will become too confused. memorise just the questions first & then, after you are comfortable enough & feel you have memorised all the questions, memorise the answers. if someone asks you a question that is not on the list of questions, say either, 'i am sorry but i cannot answer that,' or, 'at the moment,

i am sorry but i cannot provide a
comment for that.'"

needless to say, there was a joyous
celebration & nobody asked questions
they were not supposed to ask.

following the gala, we were granted
a *resting period* of three days. the
foreman said, "have fun. do whatever
you want to do."

we ate fancy dinners & read interesting
books & watched intellectual films.

ursula mantriesta showed us how to
scuba dive at night & salman wendigo
gave a powerpoint presentation on how
to start your own business.

overall, we learned a lot & the entire
three days was a good time.

at the end of the three days, the foreman produced blueprints from his bungalow & said, "this is our next project."

it was to be called, *black cube*.

there was a bit of discussion, followed by an interesting moment where the foreman appointed yassine matternack as chief construxion officer. yassine matternack then turned around & made kevelk dosche project manager & kevelk dosche, in turn, made greg batnick (formerly, a professor of fluid dynamics at a small university in barcelona) assistant project manager.

together, the three began to draw plans for one of the eight swimming pools we were to include as part of our final design for this new project.

the foreman also named jahred lindley & alexei maternel lead terraformer & original surveyor, respectively.

black magician was flown in that evening to swear them in. he left shortly after.

later, after the officiations & signing of documents, over the campfire, alexei maternel said, "i'm beginning to think this is the best job i've ever had, truly!"

a film was shown on the projector in december. a documentary documenting the 1964 summer olympics in tokyo. it was called *tokyo olympiad*. we began at sundown & by the end of the film, a crescent moon could be seen. the night sky was a mesmerizing sort of evening green.

ramon colon said a few days later, during a quick game of football[3] after lunch, "i don't underst& why they had to use slow motion & orchestral music like that. i get that it's being used as a sort of leitmotif, but for whatever reason, it really didn't gel with me."

we organized a racewalking competition after the football match & phyllis salvador won.

the prize was this new type of bar soap invented by wasiim gaultier, designed for an overall better bathing experience.

five months passed & we were almost finished with the new project. we built a functioning satellite radio tower but something went wrong.

travis martinèque, who knew about satellite radio towers, said one of his calculations had been off. "we have to start all over."

we dismantled the satellite & destroyed a few pieces in the process.

grayes armitage said, "why did we have

to start all over? now, the destroyed pieces are going to take weeks to get here. can't we just salvage & remake part of it, instead of *do nothing* but sit & wait?"

travis martinèque was not very good at explaining his craft so no one really understood what he was trying to say when he explained to grayes armitage that, "the melting point of the magnesium does not allow that we mix it with the zinc."

the very next day, black magician appeared & had lunch with us. he said, "i won't be here too long, i'm afraid."

he played football with us & then went to speak with the foreman.

before the end of the day, black

magician took travis martinèque away with him, this time in a[n] aeroplane.

the foreman appeared during dinner & introduced us to luis yaq'am & said, "luis yaq'am will be the new travis martinèque."

"i am from portugal," luis yaq'am said.

& that was that.

the next morning, once we commenced building the new satellite radio tower, already, we could tell: luis yaq'am was much more proficient at his craft than travis martinèque.

by around 2:00am, the tower was back up & this time, we were already hearing sounds from outer space.

in august, there was a day with hornets & what felt like a very dry heat.

the foreman said, "do not come out from your bunkers, there's hornets & a very dry heat."

dante peters said out loud, "but, i need my walkman," & walked out to retrieve his listening device.

the hornets were quick to get him.

the foreman cried out, but there was

nothing anyone could do.

a man in a beekeeper outfit appeared with smoke & fire & leaves.

he did this all day, the thing with smoke & fire.

it took a long time but eventually, the hornets, they went away.

& the dry heat also, it left with the hornets (& the man in the beekeeper suit).

we buried dante peters near the second well & the foreman said, "tomorrow, we have to make up for today's lost time."

after lights out, antoine fincher talked about the man with smoke & fire. he said he once knew a man who reminded him of the man with smoke & fire, & showed us this photograph:

4

we were offered one day of vacation
by the foreman so we explored nearby
caves.

we stayed out late & it was 3:32am in
september so everything looked super
beautiful.

the stars in the sky shone very
brightly.

steffan poplionovius took pictures of
the moon & focused on the reflections
of things off the surface of other

things.

reymon fantaglio said, "is that pentax or fujifilm?"

steffan poplionovius said, "no — it's olympus," & raised his camera in the moonlight, above his head, so reymon fantaglio could see the camera was in fact an olympus.

we spelunked & went cave diving & did this until maybe a little after morning. animal sounds dominated most of what was going on around us & we were tired & we knew work was supposed to start in three hours but we didn't care.

cosmatos panamos started a fire & told a story of crazed villagers & savage cannibals as we ate a breakfast of eggs & cantaloupe & waited for the

factory whistle to signal that it was
time for work.

in november, two famous men appeared.
one sang songs & the other filmed films.

the one who sang songs wore maison
kitsuné wide-leg striped stretch-
cotton seersucker shorts & a very nice
& new-looking saint laurent printed
cotton-piqué polo shirt.

the film director, who was much more
simple & elegant, wore a blue boglioli
slim-fit cotton suit.

they were making a music video for

one of the singer's songs.

they wanted us to appear in a h&ful of shots, working on what we were working on.

the singer pointed to white cube in the distance & said to the foreman, "i really enjoy the idea of white cube, it's an incredible thing."

for one week, the film director & his
crew & the singer kept stitching
together different shots while we
pretended to work, each of us, on a
section of the new project.

we were specifically told, by the film
director, "do not look at the camera."

everything felt like a party.

they used smoke machines & strobe
lights.

yves renquin even had an attack & we didn't find out until later that this was because he was an epileptic.

one of the assistants, toward the end of the shoot, made us sign release forms & arturo deville, pointing to a line on the second page said, "i can't read or write. what's that say?"

l&ing crafts appeared in early february.

paul agabbe said to the foreman, "i received a telegram from the company asking me to work another job somewhere that is someplace else, for a little more pay. i think i am going to go do it."

& at first, it was just a few people: pedro granible, thérèse jules, franc quer & ubary ra'am. (but then paul agabbe too.)

almost everyone was leaving.

then, on a monday, black magician appeared almost out of nowhere & visited with the foreman in his office for a little bit.

there was something off about black magician — something that seemed different.

almost like he wasn't the same black magician from a few months ago.

pretty much, by the end of the day, the foreman called a meeting in the lunchroom & announced the new project had officially been called off & there wouldn't be anymore funding.

he showed us a telegram to prove this & said, "ask black magician if you've any questions."

black magician was outside. he played songs & sang on the guitar he'd brought along & told a story of when he had been a young man & how he had worked very hard to make his fortune & how now he was living in south africa (where he had always wanted to be) & could never imagine living anywhere else & how he saw time as nothing but a flat circle.

after his song, simonette de gaulle said, "black magician, what happens next?"

black magician looked at simonette
de gaulle, pointed to white cube &
smiled, "do you remember what i said
to you, all those months ago?"

& in that instant, a bright light
shone from behind the structure.

the earth rumblings returned & white
cube appeared even more magnificent &
more white & more gleaming than ever
before.

black magician snapped a pic & sang
a new song & strummed a few licks on
his guitar.

simonette de gaulle began writing
things & black magician shouted
lyrics:

ti ti tiri tiri ti ti tiri tiri titi
ti ti tiri tiri ti ti tiri tiri ti ti
ti ti tiri tiri ti ti tiri tiri titi
ti ti tiri tiri ti ti tiri tiri ti ti
ti ti tiri tiri ti ti tiri tiri titi
ti ti tiri tiri ti ti tiri tiri ti ti
ti ti tiri tiri ti ti tiri tiri titi
ti ti tiri tiri ti ti tiri tiri ti ti
ti ti tiri tiri ti ti tiri tiri titi
ti ti tiri tiri ti ti tiri tiri ti ti
ti ti tiri tiri ti ti tiri tiri titi
ti ti tiri tiri ti ti tiri tiri ti ti
ti ti tiri tiri ti ti tiri tiri titi
ti ti tiri tiri ti ti tiri tiri ti ti
ti ti tiri tiri ti ti tiri tiri titi
ti ti tiri tiri ti ti tiri tiri ti ti
ti ti tiri tiri ti ti tiri tiri titi
ti ti tiri tiri ti ti tiri tiri ti ti
ti ti tiri tiri ti ti tiri tiri titi
ti ti tiri tiri ti ti tiri tiri ti ti
ti ti tiri tiri ti ti tiri tiri titi

ti ti tiri tiri ti ti tiri tiri ti ti
ti ti tiri tiri ti ti tiri tiri titi
ti ti tiri tiri ti ti tiri tiri ti ti
ti ti tiri tiri ti ti tiri tiri titi
ti ti tiri tiri ti ti tiri tiri ti ti
ti ti tiri tiri ti ti tiri tiri titi
ti ti tiri tiri ti ti tiri tiri ti ti
ti ti tiri tiri ti ti tiri tiri titi
ti ti tiri tiri ti ti tiri tiri ti ti
ti ti tiri tiri ti ti tiri tiri titi
ti ti tiri tiri ti ti tiri tiri ti ti
ti ti tiri tiri ti ti tiri tiri titi
ti ti tiri tiri ti ti tiri tiri ti ti
ti ti tiri tiri ti ti tiri tiri titi
ti ti tiri tiri ti ti tiri tiri ti ti
ti ti tiri tiri ti ti tiri tiri titi
ti ti tiri tiri ti ti tiri tiri ti ti
ti ti tiri tiri ti ti tiri tiri titi
ti ti tiri tiri ti ti tiri tiri ti ti
ti ti tiri tiri ti ti tiri tiri titi
ti ti tiri tiri ti ti tiri tiri ti ti

ti ti tiri tiri ti ti tiri tiri titi
ti ti tiri tiri ti ti tiri tiri ti ti
ti ti tiri tiri ti ti tiri tiri titi
ti ti tiri tiri ti ti tiri tiri ti ti
ti ti tiri tiri ti ti tiri tiri titi
ti ti tiri tiri ti ti tiri tiri ti ti
ti ti tiri tiri ti ti tiri tiri titi
ti ti tiri tiri ti ti tiri tiri ti ti
ti ti tiri tiri ti ti tiri tiri titi
ti ti tiri tiri ti ti tiri tiri ti ti
ti ti tiri tiri ti ti tiri tiri titi
ti ti tiri tiri ti ti tiri tiri ti ti
ti ti tiri tiri ti ti tiri tiri titi
ti ti tiri tiri ti ti tiri tiri ti ti
ti ti tiri tiri ti ti tiri tiri titi
ti ti tiri tiri ti ti tiri tiri ti ti
ti ti tiri tiri ti ti tiri tiri titi
ti ti tiri tiri ti ti tiri tiri ti ti
ti ti tiri tiri ti ti tiri tiri titi
ti ti tiri tiri ti ti tiri tiri ti ti
ti ti tiri tiri ti ti tiri tiri titi

ti ti tiri tiri ti ti tiri tiri ti ti
ti ti tiri tiri ti ti tiri tiri titi
ti ti tiri tiri ti ti tiri tiri ti ti
ti ti tiri tiri ti ti tiri tiri titi
ti ti tiri tiri ti ti tiri tiri ti ti
ti ti tiri tiri ti ti tiri tiri titi
ti ti tiri tiri ti ti tiri tiri ti ti
ti ti tiri tiri ti ti tiri tiri titi
ti ti tiri tiri ti ti tiri tiri ti ti
ti ti tiri tiri ti ti tiri tiri titi
ti ti tiri tiri ti ti tiri tiri ti ti
ti ti tiri tiri ti ti tiri tiri titi
ti ti tiri tiri ti ti tiri tiri ti ti
ti ti tiri tiri ti ti tiri tiri titi
ti ti tiri tiri ti ti tiri tiri ti ti
ti ti tiri tiri ti ti tiri tiri titi
ti ti tiri tiri ti ti tiri tiri ti ti
ti ti tiri tiri ti ti tiri tiri titi
ti ti tiri tiri ti ti tiri tiri ti ti
ti ti tiri tiri ti ti tiri tiri titi
ti ti tiri tiri ti ti tiri tiri ti ti

ti ti tiri tiri ti ti tiri tiri titi
ti ti tiri tiri ti ti tiri tiri ti ti
ti ti tiri tiri ti ti tiri tiri titi
ti ti tiri tiri ti ti tiri tiri ti ti
ti ti tiri tiri ti ti tiri tiri titi
ti ti tiri tiri ti ti tiri tiri ti ti
ti ti tiri tiri ti ti tiri tiri titi
ti ti tiri tiri ti ti tiri tiri ti ti
ti ti tiri tiri ti ti tiri tiri titi
ti ti tiri tiri ti ti tiri tiri ti ti
ti ti tiri tiri ti ti tiri tiri titi
ti ti tiri tiri ti ti tiri tiri ti ti
ti ti tiri tiri ti ti tiri tiri ti ti
ti ti tiri tiri ti ti tiri tiri titi
ti ti tiri tiri ti ti tiri tiri ti ti
ti ti tiri tiri ti ti tiri tiri titi
ti ti tiri tiri ti ti tiri tiri ti ti
ti ti tiri tiri ti ti tiri tiri titi
ti ti tiri tiri ti ti tiri tiri ti ti
ti ti tiri tiri ti ti tiri tiri titi
ti ti tiri tiri ti ti tiri tiri ti ti

ti ti tiri tiri ti ti tiri tiri titi
ti ti tiri tiri ti ti tiri tiri ti ti
ti ti tiri tiri ti ti tiri tiri titi
ti ti tiri tiri ti ti tiri tiri ti ti
ti ti tiri tiri ti ti tiri tiri titi
ti ti tiri tiri ti ti tiri tiri ti ti
ti ti tiri tiri ti ti tiri tiri titi
ti ti tiri tiri ti ti tiri tiri ti ti
ti ti tiri tiri ti ti tiri tiri titi
ti ti tiri tiri ti ti tiri tiri ti ti
ti ti tiri tiri ti ti tiri tiri titi
ti ti tiri tiri ti ti tiri tiri ti ti
ti ti tiri tiri ti ti tiri tiri titi
ti ti tiri tiri ti ti tiri tiri ti ti
ti ti tiri tiri ti ti tiri tiri titi
ti ti tiri tiri ti ti tiri tiri ti ti
ti ti tiri tiri ti ti tiri tiri titi
ti ti tiri tiri ti ti tiri tiri ti ti
ti ti tiri tiri ti ti tiri tiri titi
ti ti tiri tiri ti ti tiri tiri ti ti

as long as ropes unravel
fake rolex will travel.

n then she said i need to tell
u somethin, n dont hate me
for it...

mike practices a kind of insolence
that makes my mind twitch at times,
like i'm falling into a world that
wants to regulate itself otherly, but
not to the point of alienating itself
by being unfathomable. he populates
his work with words that often look
like he made them up, but then there
they are in the dictionary, or on
youtube, or in apple music. a lot of
them actually are made up words, just
not made up by mike. but then, all

words are made up. all words arrive in the world empty until we fill them with form, and mike's writing won't let you forget this.

just as every word is a container that comes to us empty and waits for us to fill it, so too are sentences containers, and paragraphs and chapters. what we fill them with is random, but as we continue to live and read, we forget about the randomness and come to regard words as fixed in meaning.

why does mike make a footnote of a three-word explanation that could so easily have been incorporated into the text? is it just to be funny? it is funny. it's funny because it's a spoof of what we might expect. what

we might expect is what mike wants us
to resist.

what i notice often is the punctuation.
bracketed phrases that might have
been, like the footnote mentioned
above, woven seamlessly into the text.
but i can see the seams. it's like
mike wants to show me the seams, or
more like he wants to introduce new
seams, seams that the piece wouldn't
normally even contain, hidden or not.
like some punk sewing colours into a
jean jacket.

there's no way to escape the thrust
of the narrative as it rolls forward
word by word gathering momentum, but
mike throws up brackets and colons
to make us aware of the elusiveness
of the meaning we embrace as though

by regulation. he makes us aware of our desire to escape the pain of our momentary randomness by seeing progression, the illusion of an endless motion forward into an eternity we can never contain.

so some of it is silly. monty python dressed in armani eating beans heated over a campfire out of a can pried open by a jackknife.

it's like mike is stepping forward, using his words as stepping stones he tosses out in front of him, one at a time, trying to make his way to a place he can't yet imagine. or like he's staying in one place dancing to the music in his head, trying to make us, his readers, hear his music by way of his movements.

at the point when obscure serbian
musician abul morgard begins to play
a concert, in the first part of the
book, mike's words stumble and fall
apart until the text turns into a
series of punctuation with no words
to serve it. what does music become
when words fail it? what do i become
when i have no words to tell what i'm
trying to put into words, what i'm
trying to dress up in words?

as i progress through mike's book,
i forget what i've read almost
immediately... it's like the words
he uses are porous, light, ephemeral,
turning to dust as i move forward
into a new patch of words, like
approaching of vague memory that has
slipped away enough to make me hanker
after it, to leave a sore feeling

where the emptiness sits in place of the words i continue to pursue. like a half-forgotten memory of a melody that plays in my head, but then loses coherence when i try to hum it... like a wordless sound i can't quite hear. until "it doesn't matter (to zizou) anymore what anyone has to say about music."

like sitting on the edge of a dream, where the dream side is a wash of silent images and the waking side perches on the edge of it hearing the hollow echo of words trying to snare the images, and the dream side tearing the images into pieces that float together like shards of puzzle looking for a place to connect, to settle together into something like a picture, but where the overriding

tension is a desire to hold the
pieces apart, like a magnetic force
that attracts the pieces toward each
other and makes them simultaneously
repellent. there is something repellent
in this writing, but repellent in
the strongest sense, repellent in a
manner that is attractive.

you seem comfortable amid metaphor,
mike, but you also seem to be resisting
metaphor. a book is a metaphor. it
ekes out a space in the world, it
shapes the air it occupies... but then
it accordions out into something else
altogether. the shape of it stands in
for what it becomes as it is read.
it's meaning stands beyond the shape
it occupies. the shape, what we call
'book', stands for something other
than the shape. the shape 'book'

tells us we are approaching metaphor and that tale of approach is itself already metaphor. in the same sense what we call a chapter is also a metaphor. what we call a chapter spreads itself across the pages to produce a meaning that is not the shape of the chapter. so too with each paragraph, and each sentence, and now, perhaps most evidently in your book, mike, we see that each word is a metaphor. each word stands in for something other than itself. a metaphor is a placeholder. it holds the space. it directs our gaze.

it is at the level of the word that you, mike, mount your resistance to the fact of the metaphor. you never make it all that difficult for us readers to follow along. but as we trot along the path you've set out, we are constantly tripped up, or maybe brought up short, by words that seem to have no evident or easy meaning, beyond the sort of sonorous meaning a child might assign to a word encountered for the first time.

the words in a book just disappear as you move away from them, as you move deeper into each sentence, deeper into the book. what you have read is gone, and if you go back, you come upon the words from a different direction. which means it isn't the words themselves that carry the meaning, but the direction from which you arrive to encounter the words.

zizou disappears into the music and mike's writing turns multitrack, like overdubbing the written narrative with a sonic attack. like a silencing of narrative through what is ostensibly only narrative.

it's like you are trying to outrun the words. i love the bursts of wordless punctuation, and the illustrations, and the solid black pages... then you see the words streaming out ahead of you, singing a song you can't quite catch up to, but are game always to try.

there's a moment when we readers step back into narrative and become aware of ourselves again, and we coexist with the music. it's like a wall of meaning that has no words or sound but is represented in words and sounds. the words are like sonic bricks that

look like they should mean, but mean
in a way that isn't the same as how
they look.

...

it starts with an image. black and
white. grainy. looks like the earth.
a small circle with black splotches
that look like continents. at the
bottom, it looks like the earth is
melting, dripping. there are some
words orbiting the earth: theory-
fiction, sf, a word that looks like
it might be salt, but i don't think
it is.

the next page is blank, and then
a page that is solid black with a
reverse image in the middle, like
a negative. there seems to be some

upside-down numbers at the top of the image.

the next page is solid black.

i find myself developing a kind of narrative based on what i'm seeing, even though what i'm seeing doesn't look like it constitutes any sort of narrative in a conventional sense.

there's a page with a lot of what seems to be stray punctuation dotted about on it. periods and commas. maybe they have escaped from the rest of the book.

there's a woman with a face like fire. her husband has eyes like the sky. and there's a man with ears like the galaxy.

then there is mostly a list of bands
or musicians.

...

written words embrace a kind of
silence in the reader. which is
why it is so difficult to write about
music. mike approaches this problem
by turning the music into a kind of
physical presence in the life of the
protagonist, zizou. sort of like
an acid trip where music becomes
a corporeal presence. but an acid
trip is just as hard to write about
as music. mike deals with this by
creating a fractured narrative
that wanders about in an alternate
dimension bringing zizou to the edge
of the silence that fills her with a
desire to make some noise.

i thought "klangfarbenmelodie" was a word mike just made up and tossed into the first paragraph of the book, and i was a couple of paragraphs further along when i thought: wait a minute... i better look this up. sure enough, it's one of those long german words compounded from a bunch of other smaller words, in this case, according to google, "sound-colour melody".

in the end, the silence of music defeats us in our attempts to show ourselves, to make ourselves visible, to stand behind ourselves and tell through our words what the world looks like from back here, standing back here in the silence behind our words. in the end, the silence of music shows us what our words are utterly incapable of.

as mike's book continues, the words morph. they start to become things other than what we expect, other than what we are used to. 'hands' becomes 'h&s'. and 'life' becomes 'lyfe'. is 'life' something different from 'lyfe'? if i see the word 'life' and you see the word 'life', are we seeing the same thing? our reliance on the solidness we want to perceive in the words we share makes us forget the randomness of the way we spell our words... and the way we live our lives... the way we construct our narratives. among other things, mike's book feels like an invitation to revisit this randomness, an opportunity to remember what constitutes our freedom.

...

it's raining lightly into the leaves of the trees. and i can hear it dripping onto the eaves of the houses across the way. now and then a car rolls by on the street making a sound like the surf rolling onto the shore at the beach. i'm in the backyard, reading mike's book, a reading that straddles two worlds, the world of music, sound, noise, and the world of talk, which is always going to tend toward the world of explanation, almost to the point where explanation seems impossible to escape. reading mike's book brings home this gulf between what can be expressed and what presses us back toward the silence we so often want to escape, but are able sometimes to embrace, or sink into in a way that would allow the words we utter to begin to vibrate again with this silence we are always addressing... as if words could under certain circumstances bring us forth into the world and then negate themselves, freeing us to be at ease in the silence of the void that hangs always just beyond our efforts at explanation.

. . .

the last couple pages of the first section are studded with punctuation, like mike stuttering. getting started going somewhere, then realizing he's not getting off to a good start, so trying again, realizing it probably isn't possible to get to where he's trying to go, but then trying again...

and again...

...

it's all about the noun. you name a thing and it evokes a certain response in the reader. mike resists this simple equivalency that facilitates the easy access to meaning that much conventional writing seems to aim for — as though the goal of writing should be to try to get the words out of the way so as to ease the reader's passage. mike resists this tendency. and when a simple familiar detail like a powerpoint presentation, or scuba diving lessons appears amid the stream of strange nounification, it feels like arriving at a tiny desert island and standing on solid ground before jumping back onto the raft to plunge again through turbulent waters so dark as to be almost inscrutable, but also playful on the surface, the way an ocean might be on a sunny breezy day.

at the end of the book, black magician sings, and the book literally fades out. the text becomes lighter and lighter until it's very hard to read. and then it just runs off the end of the page, mid-sentence. and then i understand what makes mike's writing so attractive to me. it's because the way he structures his work is like a pop tune, but a really good one... good for me meaning one from the late 1960s or early 70s.

the pop songs of the late 60s and early 70s, the best of them, are full of catchy little hooks that threaten to become cliché, but resist cliché by banding together in surprising progressions, with strange little flourishes, and mixes that are enchantingly off-kilter, almost wrong by modern standards. mike's book is like that. you encounter all these little narrative hooks, but the way they are arranged, the way they encounter one another in passing, the way they wander and float and land and take off again, creates... well – it turns out that reading mike's book is like encountering a sound-colour melody... a kind of literary klangfarbenmelodie.

ken sparling.

with amusing zany memorable protagonist names such as zizou, abul mogard, bloodrip.exe, pippin quell, ramon colon, and beach babi and "a woman with a face like fire," mike kleine is taking the serbia of the interview process and music writing to astronomical depths. you will need "ears like the galaxy" or eyes like a gas giant to be able to see the intense social critique, spellbinding music of kleine's storytelling and migratory explorations within quantum space and coding machine.

despite the colossal fullness of kleine's wu wu wu-tang and kuedo and miscrostoria and mf doom zipcoding the incorporeal geography of pop culture, name dropping, ambient musical gobbledygook/dissonance to vatican shadow or steve hauschildt heights, kleine's work is laced and transmogrified with metaphysical sadness/expansiveness and speaks towards a "stench of ambient decay" and "traumatized [hyper]irreality." this is to say that there is no parallel universe nor intergalactic space as macro-potent or as intra-warped or as radiating so sub-atomically as the one that exists in kleine's magnificent and delightfully exciting imagination.

<u>vi khi nao.</u>

some of us call magick love, but we are mistaken. some of us call magick coincidence, but we are mistaken. some of us call magick god, but we are mistaken. magick is inchoate, incomplete, underneath everything and impacts upon everything that we do. magick is the abyss, the text laid upon the page. everything in between is us.

...

<u>_third world magicks_</u> is a book possessed by the underworld spirit of the green screen. the protagonist is (apparently) blank zizou, a canvas projected onto by digital entities and acclaimed musicians and empty space. this is mike kleine at his comedic best, a literary mirage of ironic illusions and surfaces. i realised early that it was funny, but i only started laughing once i recast myself as a person in the real world, this 'other place,' whatever that means, outside kleine's 'text,' once i felt myself in blank's shoes, written upon, written over, transforming into a black magician speaking with a distinct hollywood accent, almost like i'm a modern-day screenwriter, living in relation to mediating technologies and deconstructing

threads, yes, like _third world magicks_ itself. i slipped between the name i own and the name i am given, because this is a book that teaches you how to read it. it is possible to imagine the existence of other things than this once we accept that the world is constituted of things other than this. that's magick.

. . .

written in taut, sparse prose, mike kleine's _third world magicks_ resembles the great 21st century masterworks of pynchon and delillo, what with their artists in disarray, their silly names, their too many metaphors, their ontological instability, their mirroring, their lots of white space on the page, their almost resembling an airport paperback, not in a derogatory sense, in an intellectual one, like, imagine you're waiting for a flight and among the racks of overpriced chocolate and shitty sunglasses and right there, just right there, there's a whole host of books and they all have corporate gloss on the cover, except for this one book which is pretty plain, actually, it just says magicien noir three times (or maybe it says bleeding edge, or the silence), and you don't actually have the brain cells left (because of the stopover jet lag) to translate that to "black magician" in your brain, and actually, you're not sure that's what it means anyhow, but, whatever, it has a pretty plain and relaxing purple cover, so you pick it up and buy it, and so does everyone else in the airport, and it becomes a new york times bestseller, people sleep with it in their hands on the plane, it's a talisman, it quite literally creates magick in the world around it, it is a surface that people rest their heads on to go to sleep, they dream over it, or spill coffee on it, or, in rare cases, they might pick it up and read, engage in deeply, scribble over the white space, stare into the white space and work out some shit about themselves they'd been hiding for a while, or, in truly truly rare cases, like, even rarer than rare, they might read and engage deeply, stare into the black text, become possessed by magick, not just on the surface but underneath it too, spouting a bunch of words, laughing in their own face, taking stock, saying seeya later, writing a book of their own, a much worse one, which somehow sells even better, but by whose metrics? what matters? who am i anyway? who's that mike kleine guy again? and why is magic spelled with a k? what is this? wait, i was meant to read it? like, over a long period of time? what is this anyway? where am i? i have a flight to catch? what? what?

<u>josiah morgan.</u>

a drop-kick right up the cerebellum!

<u>jon chandler.</u>

there's no other way to explain how kleine creates atmosphere — he is translating something outside of language and putting it into language, through the experience of very ordinary people doing ordinary things. _third world magicks_ gives us the experience of the exceptional through the vessel of the banal. i'm not sure if this is irony or if it is just what is true to the human experience, maybe it is both. the one thing i am sure of is _third world magicks_ is a synesthetic masterpiece.

<u>elle nash.</u>

appendix

appendix

---

[1] verklempt

[2] *magicien noir*

[3] soccer in some countries

[4] https://thispersondoesnotexist.com

www.ingramcontent.com/pod-product-compliance
Lightning Source LLC
Chambersburg PA
CBHW040904010826
48978CB00013BB/1146